To
ANYONE WHO IS HAVING A BAD DAY

Copyright © 2016 Philip C. Stead

A Neal Porter Book

Published by Roaring Brook Press

Roaring Brook Press is a division of Holtzbrinck Publishing Holdings Limited Partnership

175 Fifth Avenue, New York, New York 10010

The artwork for this book was handmade using oil pastels, charcoal, and cardboard printing.

mackids.com

All rights reserved

Library of Congress Control Number: 2016004883

ISBN 978-1-62672-182-1

Our books may be purchased in bulk for promotional, educational, or business use. Please
contact your local bookseller or the Macmillan Corporate and Premium Sales Department
at (800) 221-7945 ext. 5442 or by e-mail at MacmillanSpecialMarkets@macmillan.com.

First edition 2016

Book design by Philip C. Stead

Printed in China by RR Donnelley Asia Printing Solutions Ltd.,
Dongguan City, Guangdong Province

1   3   5   7   9   10   8   6   4   2

SAMSON
in the
SNW

PHILIP C. STEAD

A NEAL PORTER BOOK
ROARING BROOK PRESS
NEW YORK

ON SUNNY DAYS Samson tended his dandelion patch.
Stepping carefully, he used his long trunk to pull up bothersome weeds.
When he was finished he stood in the sunshine, hoping for a friend to
come along.

Samson waited quietly with his flowers to keep him company.

"Hello," said a little red bird one day.

"Oh, hello," said Samson, making cheerful conversation.

"Would you mind," asked the bird, "if I took some flowers for a friend? He is having a bad day, and his favorite color is yellow."

"Yellow is my favorite color, too," answered Samson. He chose three of his best flowers and gathered them into a bouquet for the bird.

Samson watched the little red bird fly away. He wondered what it would be like to have a friend. As he wondered he grew tired. And before realizing it, before meaning to, Samson fell into a deep and lumbering sleep.
He dreamed of the color yellow.

While Samson slept, angry clouds came and covered up the sun. The wind began to blow, and very soon all the warmth of the day was gone.

Snow began to fall. It whirled around and around. Heavy wet clumps collected in Samson's great mass of fur till he was almost completely covered up.

In Samson's dream, yellow turned to white.
That was when Samson woke.

All around, the world was different from before. Samson could hardly tell what was where and where was what. Every direction was white snow.

Samson worried about the little red bird. "I wonder if she is out there?" he thought. "I wonder if she is cold?"

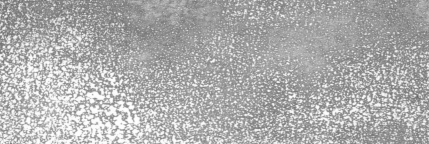

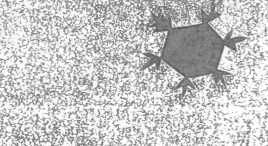

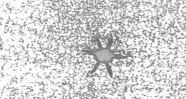

Samson stared hard into the blinding snow. "It is better to walk than to worry," he decided. And so he did.

Samson trudged through valleys and over rolling hills. The wind
blew the snow into fantastic shapes—but Samson did not stop to look.
"The little red bird is not made for this kind of weather," he thought.

Samson swung his tail and stomped his feet to free the ice that clung to his coat.

"Excuse me, please," called a mouse, mostly hidden in a snowdrift. "I would not like to be crushed."

"Oh," said Samson. "I did not see you. You should not be out here all alone."

"I know," sighed the mouse. "I did not expect a storm. I am having a bad day."

"Would you like to come with me?" asked Samson.

Grateful and relieved, the mouse made the long journey up Samson's trunk, past his vast ears, and under his thick blankets of fur. There he kept warm.

"Are you comfortable?" asked Samson.

"Oh, yes," said the mouse. "Very much so."

"I am looking for someone," said Samson. "She is small, like you."

"If she is small," said the mouse, "then we should watch where we step."

"I am looking for someone, too," said the mouse. "I worry she is having a bad day, like me. I worry she is covered up in snow."

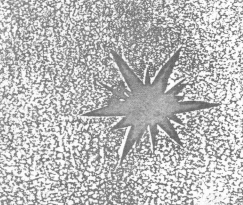

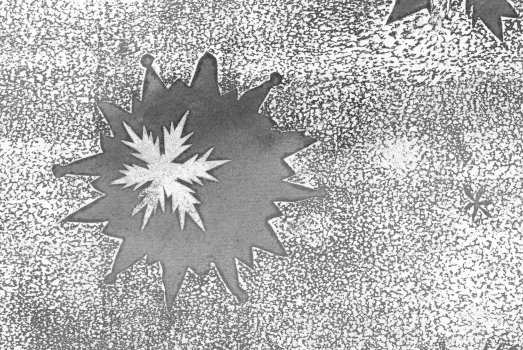

The wind howled and the snow piled higher and higher. Samson breathed deeply in and out, in and out. He stopped to rest near an unlikely patch of dandelions. "Do you have a favorite color?" he asked the mouse.

"Oh, yes." said the mouse. "My favorite color is yellow."

"Yellow is my favorite color, too," said Samson.

He reached down and gently plucked the dandelions from the snow.

"I found you!" cried Samson.

"And I found you, too!" cried the mouse.

The little red bird was too cold to reply.

"It's okay," said Samson. "I know a place not far from here."

He tucked the little red bird safely away and continued on.

Samson's passengers hopped down onto the dry cave floor.

"Thank you," said the little red bird. She shook the snow from her feathers.

"And look," she said to the mouse. "I brought you flowers!"

"Oh," said the mouse, "that is exactly what I needed today."

The three friends huddled together and told stories of their adventures in the snow.

Not long from then, the storm passed.

THE END